Emily Arnold McCully

SCHOOL

Harper & Row, Publishers

School

Library of Congress Cataloging-in-Publication Data
McCully, Emily Arnold.
  School.

  Summary: A curious little mouse decides to find out
what school is all about.
  [1. Mice—Fiction.   2. Schools—Fiction.
3. Stories without words]   I. Title.
PZ7.M478415Sc 1987   [E]   87-156
ISBN 0-06-024132-2
ISBN 0-06-024133-0 (lib. bdg.)

For Harriet

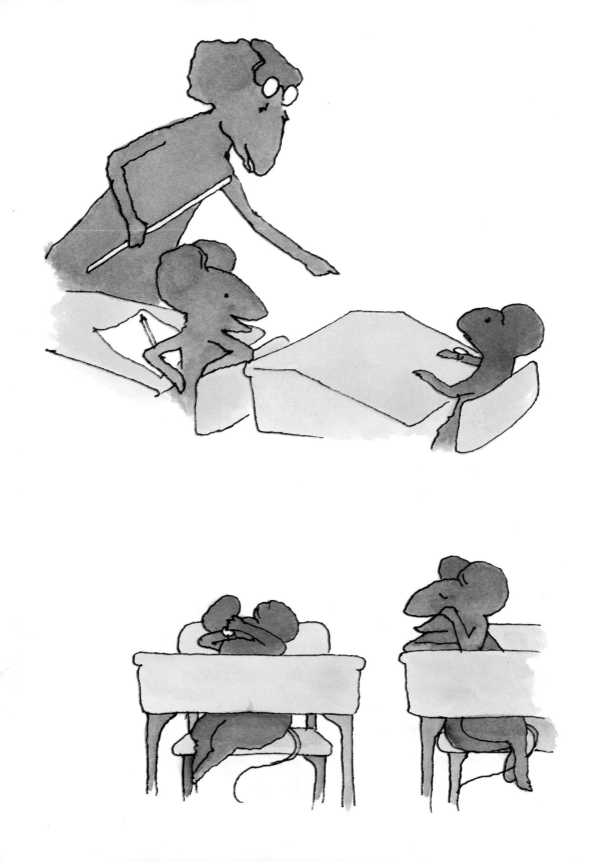

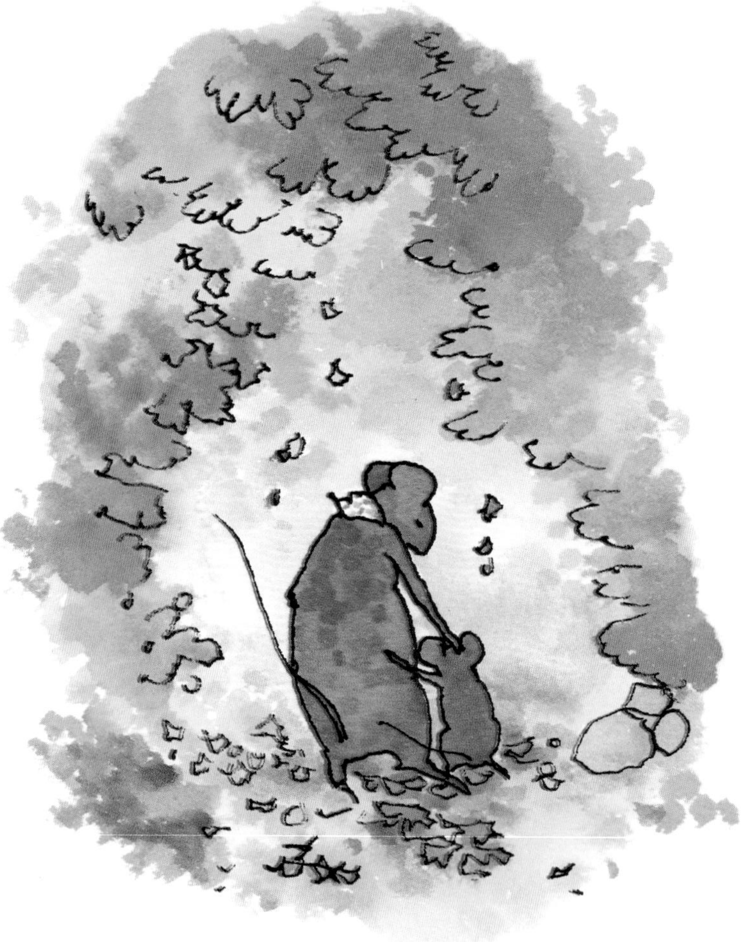